This book
is dedicated to my
Grandpa Dan, who
loved me so much
and believed I could
accomplish anything
I wanted. Thank you
for believing in me.
I love you!

Designed by Flowerpot Press
www.FlowerpotPress.com
DJS-0810-0199 ∗ 978-1-4867-2110-8
Made in China/Fabriqué en Chine

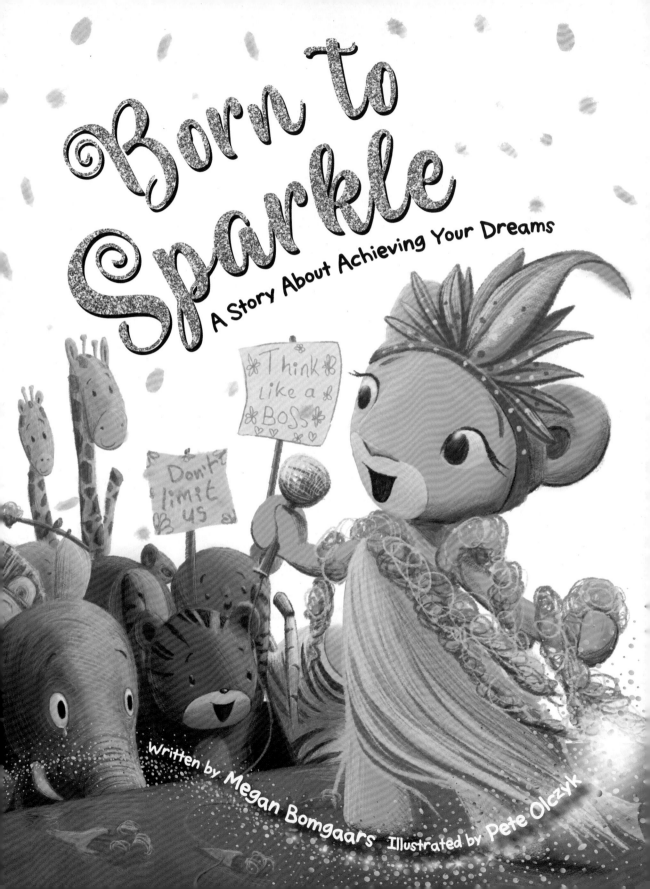

Born to Sparkle
A Story About Achieving Your Dreams

Think like a BOSS

Don't limit us

Written by Megan Bomgaars Illustrated by Pete Olczyk

I just love to **sparkle!**

I want everyone to sparkle with me!
We are all born to let our sparkle shine!

We are all born to
love and to be loved.

So show your love.

Share your love.

Sparkle!

The best way to sparkle is to live your dreams.
You sparkle when you dream your dreams and
share them with the world!

Make sure you dream BIG!
You can be a FIREFIGHTER or a DANCER.

You can be an ACTOR or a DOCTOR.

You can be a TEACHER or a CHEF or a HOMECOMING KING!

You can be anything you want.
You can do anything you want.
If you can dream it, you can do it.

You can
sparkle.

There
are no
limits.

Anything is possible.

Don't limit yourself.

There is just one thing
you need to know first...

I can and I will

If you really want to follow your dreams and if you really want to show your sparkle, then you need to work.

You need to work hard.

Dreams are not like wishes. You can't just wish upon a star and then wait. Dreams are about working hard and doing your best to make them happen.

To make your dreams come true, you need to go for it.

You have to
be brave.

You
have
to ask
questions.

You have to
study and learn.

And you
have to
practice.

Big dreamers
make their
dreams
come true.

You can do this.

You can dream big and
you can live your dreams.

It is all possible because...

You are born to sparkle!

Now it is time to really start showing the world all the light that is inside of you.

It is time for you

Born to Sparkle

A TV personality, public speaker, artist, and entrepreneur, Megan Bomgaars is a leader in the Down syndrome community. The 27-year-old starred on A&E's Emmy Award-winning and Critics' Choice Real TV Award-winning reality television show *Born This Way*.

In 2013, Megan embarked on a school project that later became the launch to her career as a Down syndrome activist. Working with her teachers, she created a film called "Don't Limit Me," aimed to demonstrate how individuals with disabilities thrive from inclusive learning environments. The video went viral, leading to Megan receiving requests to speak at events all over the world.

Megan has presented at the NDSC Annual Convention in front of thousands of people, been invited to the White House to attend first lady Michelle Obama's Beating the Odds Summit, represented the Global Down Syndrome Foundation at several conferences, and became a Quincy Jones Exceptional Advocacy Awardee and a Global Down Syndrome Foundation Spokesperson. Megan also gave a heartfelt speech at Global's Grand Opening Ceremony of their new headquarters and a keynote presentation at the Trisomy 21 Research International Conference in Barcelona, Spain.

Megan engages her community with a strong social media presence, coining the hashtags #DontLimitMe and #BeautyHasNoLimits. She also maintains the website megology.com. Utilizing her digital platform and her artistic skills, Megan develops and sells a variety of products, including customized scarves and tote bags. Megan has been featured in the Sephora "We Belong to Something Beautiful" campaign and has teamed up with Sanrio's Hello Kitty to create a fashionable clothing line.

Megan is currently attending college and studying communications and film studies.

Follow Megan on Instagram @meganbomgaars!